DATE DUE

	JAN 2 1 2012		

DEMCO 128-5046

Heart to Heart

George Shannon

Illustrated by Steve Björkman

Houghton Mifflin Company
Boston 1995

Library of Congress Cataloging-in-Publication Data

Shannon, George.
Heart to Heart / by George Shannon ; illustrated by Steve
Björkman.
p.   cm.
Summary: Upset that he has forgotten a valentine for his friend
Mole, Squirrel starts to make a fancy card but discovers a better
gift.
ISBN 0-395-72773-1
[1. Valentine's Day—Fiction.   2. Squirrels—Fiction.   3. Moles
(Animals)—Fiction.   4. Friendship—Fiction.   5. Memory—Fiction.]
I. Björkman, Steve, ill.   II. Title.
PZ7. S5287He   1995   94-36589
[E]—dc20   CIP
                             AC

Printed in the United States of America

WOZ   10   9   8   7   6   5   4   3   2   1

For Kate McIntyre

— G.S.

For nieces and nephews

Björkman, Gross, McSunas, and Sjodin

— S.B.

Squirrel got a big valentine in the mail.

Dear Squirrel,

HAPPY VALENTINE'S DAY !
I'm bringing a cake for us to share at noon.

Your best friend,
Mole

"Uh oh," said Squirrel. "This is awful.
I've been so busy I completely forgot!"

Squirrel grabbed his crayons, paper, and pens.

"Wait! Better yet. If I make it fancy he'll never guess I forgot."

Squirrel got glitter, brushes, and glue. Ran back to his desk.
"Wait! Better yet. Ribbons will make it twice as good.
He'll never ever guess I forgot."

Squirrel got the ribbons. Ran back to his desk.
"Wait! Better yet. A friend like Mole deserves the best!"

Squirrel ran to get yarn and his paper punch.
Ran back to his desk. "Wait! Better yet."

Got rickrack, felt, and crepe paper, too.
"Wait! Better yet."

Got lace, confetti, and a red balloon.
"Wait! Better yet."

Squirrel was running to the attic for his twinkle lights
when he suddenly stopped.
"Uh oh. Now WHERE did I leave my scissors last?"

Squirrel looked in every drawer in his desk.

Looked in the cupboards, his dresser, and beneath his bed.

Looked in the woodpile, sofa, and trash.

He looked everywhere, but the scissors weren't there.
Though he *did* find a mitten he'd lost last year.

"This is awful," said Squirrel. "And terrible, too!
I forget everything. I'd forget my tail if it wasn't so big.
Now I won't have any valentine for mole."

Squirrel looked at the mitten he'd found and groaned.
"It's not even mine.
It's one of the four that *Mole* lost last year!"

Squirrel laughed. "Maybe *that's* why we're best good friends. We both forget. Like the time we got lost hiking 'cause both of us forgot our maps. And the time—"

Squirrel stopped and grinned. "Maybe I don't forget *everything*."

He ran to the dresser and grabbed a stick that coiled like a snake.
Then ran to the cupboard for a cracker box.

Ran to the trash for a jelly lid. Punched it full of holes.
Then ran to the closet for a pack of seeds.

Ran to the box underneath his bed for a purple button
and an old postcard of a sailing ship.

Squirrel danced as he went from room to room,
gluing each new thing in place.

"Better yet. Better yet!"

He'd just glued the bird he'd saved from
his birthday cake when Mole arrived.

"HAPPY VALENTINE'S DAY!"

Mole stared with his mouth open wide.
"It's...It's the stick we thought was a hungry snake
when we forgot our maps on the hiking trip?"

"Like it?" asked Squirrel.
Mole slowly smiled as he stared even more.
"It's the most beautiful valentine I've ever seen!"

"See the marble?" said Squirrel.
"From the time we went to the beach," said Mole, "and dropped our lunch in the sand. And the firefly lid!"

Squirrel nodded with a grin. "All stories nobody knows but us."